When Spring Comes

When Spring Comes

BY Kevin Henkes

ILLUSTRATED BY Laura Dronzek

SCHOLASTIC INC.

ISBN 978-1-338-19625-2

12 11 10 9 8 7 6 5 4 3 2 1   17 18 19 20 21 22

Printed in the U.S.A.   08

First Scholastic printing, March 2017

Acrylic paints were used to prepare the full-color art.
The text type is Bernhard Gothic SG Medium.

For Will and Clara

Before Spring comes,
the trees look like
black sticks against the sky.

But if you wait,
Spring will bring
leaves and blossoms.

If you wait, Spring will make
the leftover mounds of snow smaller

and smaller

and smaller

until suddenly—

they're gone.

Before Spring comes, the grass is brown.

But if you wait, Spring will turn it green
and add little flowers.

If you wait,

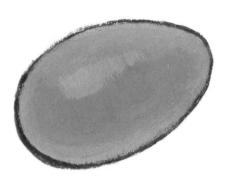

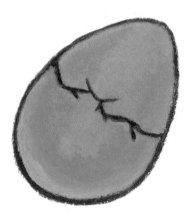

an egg will become a bird.

A seed will start growing.

Spring comes with sun

and it comes with rain.

And more rain

and more rain.

Do you like mud?
Do you like puddles?

I hope you like umbrellas.

Before Spring comes, the garden is just dirt, and empty.

But if you wait, Spring will push green shoots through the dirt to fill up the garden.

And Spring will call out the pussy willows

and new kittens, too.

Spring can come quickly or slowly.

It changes its mind a lot.

But when Spring is finally here to stay,
you will know it. . . .

There will be buds
and bees
and boots
and bubbles.

There will be worms
and wings
and wind
and wheels.

You will feel it.
You will smell it.
You will hear it.

When Spring is finally here to stay,
you might think you are done waiting,
but you are not. . . .

Now, you have to wait for Summer.

KEVIN HENKES and LAURA DRONZEK collaborated on the acclaimed picture books *Birds* and *Oh!* They live with their children in Madison, Wisconsin. Kevin Henkes is the award-winning creator of many books for children, including *Waiting*, the Caldecott Medal Winner *Kitten's First Full Moon*, the Newbery Honor Books *The Year of Billy Miller* and *Olive's Ocean*, and several best-selling books about mice, including *Lilly's Purple Plastic Purse* and *Chrysanthemum*. Laura Dronzek is a painter whose work has been exhibited nationally. Her picture books include *Moonlight*, by Helen V. Griffith; *It Is Night*, by Phyllis Rowand; and *White Is for Blueberry*, by George Shannon.